SHINE, BABY, SHINE

Leslie Staub

Illustrated by Lori Nichols

BOYDS MILLS PRESS

AN IMPRINT OF BOYDS MILLS & KANE

New York

Baby, you came into this world
with a mighty light inside.

Glorious, gleaming, miraculous, beaming . . .

Let it shine,

shine, shine.

Let it shine!

Look, baby, look!
You were born to see.
Yellow! Red! Purple! Green!

Things with wings, things that sing!
Magnificent, magical, mysterious things.

See them shine, shine, shine!
See them shine.

Listen, baby, listen!
Hear that joyful sound?
Laughter ringing, voices singing!

Quack!

Woof!

A thousand ways of saying

"I . . . love . . . you!"

Let them shine, shine, shine.
Let them shine.

Love, baby, love!
Feel it all around.
From the top of your head
to your tippy-tippy toes—
baby, you were born to love.

Let it shine, shine, shine!
Let it shine.

Fly, baby, fly!
Fly on wings of love.

Snuggle in my arms and
dream, baby, dream!
You were born to dream—

of a world so big and bright,
so filled with loving light . . .

of a world where every little light can

shine, baby, shine!

Your light, my light,
ten billion mighty little lights,
shining side by side . . .

Goodnight, little light,

sweet dreams, sleep tight!

May you shine, shine, shine!

May you shine!

For Keith Werhan
who fills my heart with light
—LS

For my wonderful agent Joanna Volpe
and shiny little Henry
—LN

For information about permission to reproduce selections
from this book, please contact permissions@bmkbooks.com.

Boyds Mills Press
An Imprint of Boyds Mills & Kane
boydsmillspress.com
Printed in China

ISBN: 978-1-59078-931-5
Library of Congress Control Number: 2019939434

First edition
10 9 8 7 6 5 4 3 2 1

Design by Barbara Grzeslo
The text is set in Neutraface.
The illustrations are created through a
digital collage of watercolor, ink, pencil,
and scanned photography.